DARK SECRETS
Of
HIDDEN MAGIC

IMA Y

authorHOUSE

AuthorHouse™ UK
1663 Liberty Drive
Bloomington, IN 47403 USA
www.authorhouse.co.uk
Phone: 0800 047 8203 (Domestic TFN)
*   +44 1908 723714 (International)*

Published by AuthorHouse 11/14/2019

ISBN: 978-1-7283-9572-2 (sc)
ISBN: 978-1-7283-9573-9 (hc)
ISBN: 978-1-7283-9571-5 (e)

—

CHAPTER 1

THE BEGINNING OF A GREAT ADVENTURE

Mr and Mrs James—number 7 Glumly Road—were a proud and normal family. They went to their usual and normal jobs, they followed their perfect and normal routines, and their kids went to a perfectly normal school. They had five children: Lily, Ana, Layla, Kaylie, and Edward James. Mr James had a nice, well-organised family. Edward was not at all good or organised, which Mr James could not tolerate. He often grounded Edward. Ana and Layla argued nonstop about whose bag was prettier or whose nails looked more stunning as they had different opinions on beauty. But twins Lily and

Kaylie were different. They were very close and hardly ever argued, unlike Ana and Layla, or got into trouble, unlike Edward.

Mr James was very strict and had many rules. One was never to let the children stay up late. But he broke his rules all the time, like don't eat the last few boxes of chocolates reserved for guests. This rule, however, was kept for Edward, and once Mr James finished all the chocolate, he blamed it on Edward. That made Mrs James angry.

Mrs James was also strict. She had a great secret that she never told anyone, including her husband. She had kept this secret since she was eleven years old, the same age as Lily and Kaylie. She got lost on her way to school. She encountered a large cave swarming with beautiful and rare multicoloured gemstones. The cave led to a hidden world of extraordinary creatures. They were surrounded by great houses and a large building safeguarded by mighty alicorns and long-tailed phoenixes, stopping Mrs James where she stood.

When she was able to move again, she approached the building. Butterflies of every colour flapped their gorgeous and delicate wings into another dimension. As many great and unbelievable scenes occurred at the same time, there was a loud deafening roar. Large groups of fierce, fiery dragons appeared out of nowhere. They charged towards the great unknown building, sending it tumbling down in tears of dark flames. As Mrs James didn't know what was going on, she headed straight for the exit and found her way back.

But Mrs James already knew that this wasn't the end of it. Especially when Mr James told her where they would soon be moving.

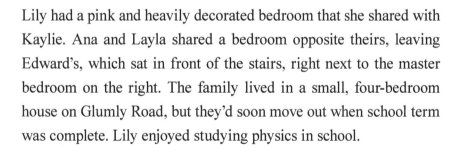

CHAPTER 2

LONDON

Lily had a pink and heavily decorated bedroom that she shared with Kaylie. Ana and Layla shared a bedroom opposite theirs, leaving Edward's, which sat in front of the stairs, right next to the master bedroom on the right. The family lived in a small, four-bedroom house on Glumly Road, but they'd soon move out when school term was complete. Lily enjoyed studying physics in school.

Only one week of school remained, and then Lily would get to spend the rest of summer with her three loveable sisters—and, of course, her irritating brother. She wasn't looking forward to spending time with Edward because he had ruined her last birthday. He dropped a handful of slimy snails and worms in her birthday cake. He also pranked her by switching the shampoo bottle with his new and improved conditioner made from muddy water; crushed-up worms; and thick, silky spiderwebs with dead spiders. These were the top-two worst things he had done to her, and they reminded her how depressing it would be with him in the house.

Lily's birthday was coming closer and closer every second. Obviously she'd share it with Kaylie, so it was often difficult to determine who to invite. Lily hoped that Edward would not interfere with her big day by playing one of his annoying, harmful jokes. She expected Ana and Layla to notice Edward's antics.

It was time for the big day; they were moving to the great and big city of London. Lily, Kaylie, and the others were excited, but they were not as excited as Edward. He'd been waiting all day to judge the size of the city. They climbed aboard Mr James's car after what seemed like many long months of packing, which they would soon get to unpack.

Hours and hours passed, and it seemed they were nowhere closer to London. They were coming from near Scotland, which was several hours from London. There was no sign of life in the dark grey car. Boredom had set in as they passed tree after tree. No one dared to speak as they knew Mrs James would come up with a few boring games to pass the journey.

The family arrived at their new home on a hot, dry, and sticky day. Each family member carried in boxes filled with teapots, electronics, books, and flowerpots. And toys, which were mostly Edward's. They also carried sofas, tables, chairs, and numerous other items. Everyone helped unpack.

When they finally finished unpacking, it was time to unwind and relax. The entire family was ready to exchange exhaustion for relief, and most took a nap. As the clock struck three, Kaylie and Lily decided it was time to head out and explore the place. Everyone else was still fast asleep. Minutes later they found themselves out and in front of their house, ready to venture into the wild.

Kaylie spotted a narrow path surrounded by tall trees the size of skyscrapers. Dark green bushes with poisonous berries lined the path. This was one mysterious and tempting adventure, as the girls had several questions. Where might the path lead? Who might be waiting at the end of the path? While Kaylie had always wanted to explore abandoned areas, Lily was a bit more cautious. She wanted to head back, especially when she saw a dark grey fence with fresh blood on it and a deep scratch through it.

"Kaylie, there could be danger lurking in there. Let's head back and find another spot," Lily said with a great shudder.

"No way! Are you serious? We just found a great place to explore." Kaylie was unable to hide her disappointment.

"Fine then. But only for a short while," Lily agreed but quickly realised she's made a complete mistake by agreeing with Kaylie.

Endlessly walking, they dodged dark oak trees in their path. They hopped over large, spongy bushes hiding tiny little ants, and they avoided sinking into dark, murky puddles. After a while, the muddy path faded away. Tall grass grew in its place, reaching up to Lily's knees. As they went deeper into the forest, they encountered a large cave overflowing with bright gems and bright shiny ores leading towards an indistinct land.

CHAPTER 3

AN UNEXPLORED LAND

Moments later they found their way to a new world, but it wasn't as pretty as the bright jewels laying naturally in the shiny grey cave. The emerald-green colour had faded away as they drew closer and closer. There was a large pile of bricks on the deserted ground. No insects or butterflies hovered around them.

Life had mysteriously drained away here. There were no signs of sunlight, only thunderclouds and constant anger.

"What happened here?" Lily asked solemnly.

"We must search for clues," Kaylie answered with a hint of suspicion.

"Okay, but we should head home soon."

They gave up after a few minutes of searching. This mystery was impossible to solve. There was no evidence of what happened. And it was impossible to solve anything by just looking through the big lumps of ash. It was as if the evidence had been burned to smithereens.

"Let's check over there," Kaylie shouted, making sure Lily had heard her as she was far away.

As they approached their destination, they found a large sword lying flat on the ground alongside a destroyed building, gleaming with a beam of light. This was the only sign of life in the unexplored area.

While the two girls argued over whether to take it, a deep voice emanated from the sword. "The sword, Excalibur, has chosen you two to save Magicland by defeating the dragon king and restoring magic to the people. Unlock the magic potential within yourselves and within this sword by imagining that you have saved this land. If you succeed, I will grant you one wish. You must not tell anyone your mission."

As the great voice faded away, the girls felt a mix of bewilderment and excitement. Lily looked as though she was about to pass out.

"Is this really true? Cool! Now we need to unlock the sword's potential. Are you in?" Kaylie spoke as if she'd known magic existed for years.

Lily was in shock. "Let's head back home." There was a tremor in her voice as she heard a howl in the distance.

"What was that?" Kaylie whispered.

"I don't know, and I don't want to know. Which way is home?" Lily bellowed as she ran.

The sisters ran in different directions. They heard a loud roar, and a fiery dragon appeared in the distance. "Yes, I am the dragon king, and I don't like intruders—particularly human ones. It's rather easy to catch humans because they have no magic. They are no match for me."

As the dragon king spoke, Kaylie hid Excalibur behind her back.

"Come on, slaves, do your jobs! Get them!" the dragon king ordered. From what seemed out of nowhere, other dragons rushed to the girls. Seconds later Kaylie and Lily were locked in a cage with a few slaves and the beaming sword.

CHAPTER 4

THE GREAT ESCAPE

After a tasteless breakfast in the dragon tower's prison, it was time to think of an escape plan. They would need a great deal of help. Lily and Kaylie shared the prison with two others who once guarded Magicland, but they were now prisoners as well.

"Are you humans?" a woman in white armour asked. She had bright wings and a shiny horn.

"Yes, we are," Lily answered. This armoured woman made her curious.

"We are the guardians of Magicland, and we can transform into winged creatures. I'm a phoenix, and she's an alicorn. My name is Ali," explained a man in red, orange, and yellow armour. He also had huge mighty wings that could probably fly up to space and beyond in seconds.

"I'm Fiona," said the woman with excitement as she saw the sword Kaylie clutched in her hand.

"I'm Kaylie, and this is Lily."

"Have you tried breaking out?" Lily asked after the guards passed by.

"You'd be crazy to do that here. There are real dragons out there, lurking in the shadows, listening to every conversation there is," Ali muttered.

"What's that?" Fiona asked with deep interest as she looked at the sword.

But before Kaylie could answer, there was a crash on the floor and a shout. "You did that on purpose, didn't you? You nearly killed me with the water. You'll be punished for this, servant," the dragon king bellowed.

The sound of a big, heavy, and loud dragon steps drowned out the rest of his speech. And they couldn't see what was going on when the large, fire-breathing dragon blocked their view.

"Told you," Ali reminded them.

"Wait, did he just say the water nearly killed him?" Lily asked. And she immediately started to create a great plan inside her head.

"That gives me an idea," Kaylie whispered as she imagined a plan to save Magicland.

After a long time arguing, they finally came up with a perfect plan and convinced the others to help. Lily and Kaylie figured that if they unlocked the hidden powers of the great sword, it might help them defeat the dragon king. The only problem was they didn't know how to unlock its hidden powers. If they couldn't, they'd have to find some water and use it to defeat the dragon king. It was as simple as that. Or was it really that simple? There had been no sign of water anywhere except at breakfast.

After many attempts to unlock the sword's potential, Lily wanted to give up. But she had another great idea.

"Does anyone have any water left?" Lily asked.

"Yes, why?" Fiona answered, a bit puzzled.

"Because if it burns the dragon king, it might burn the floor," Lily answered with intelligent logic. When the guard was out of sight, she tried her idea. Lily poured drops of water on the dungeon floor. When she was done, there was a small hole on the floor. It got bigger every second.

"You see, as simple as that," Lily whispered while the hole grew larger and larger. Finally, it was big enough for all of them to squeeze through.

As they were about to leave, the sword of magic started gleaming. A spark of light shone above it, tearing apart the prison and freeing the people of Magicland. But that wasn't the end of the dragon king as he wanted real revenge on them.

CHAPTER 5

UNDISCLOSED POWER

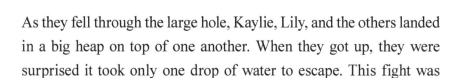

As they fell through the large hole, Kaylie, Lily, and the others landed in a big heap on top of one another. When they got up, they were surprised it took only one drop of water to escape. This fight was going to be easy. Or was it?

After what seemed like several minutes, they heard a big, mean-sounding shout coming from where the prison tower used to be. It alarmed all of them as they had no place to hide. They searched around, and Kaylie spotted a small wooden cabin standing stiff in the tall wavy grass hidden deep in the cave. It looked as if it had been there for over a thousand years. "In there," Kaylie cried, pointing to the old cabin.

Following Kaylie's lead, they stayed hidden in the dark cave, watching as the dragon king passed them and faded into the distance.

"Good thinking, Kaylie," Fiona exclaimed with a happy tone.

"Thanks," Kaylie said, admiring herself.

"Now we need to figure out how to activate this thing," Ali whispered as he gazed at Excalibur with interest as its large shiny body rested on the ground, ready to use.

"In here," Lily bellowed with a whisper—if that was really possible.

The others followed Lily into the abandoned cabin. Ali briefly hesitated. He sensed there was a big trap in the cabin, and something bad was going to happen.

They moved quietly into the antique and completely deserted house. Over time, fragments of hardened wood had chipped off the floorboard as well as the furniture. The house was devastated. And it looked as if someone had broken in and rummaged through it for a diamond or some other expensive and gorgeous jewel. The house had been turned upside down.

Fiona spotted a pair of red eyes and a tall figure in the dark shadows. It came closer and closer. "Ali, Lily, Kaylie," screamed Fiona. She attempted to fly but couldn't as the king of dragons had drained the power from her.

"Her voice came from this way," Lily whispered, leading the way. She had to watch her steps as sharp tools, such as daggers, appeared out of nowhere.

Out of the corner of Fiona's eye she spotted a small piece of paper. Curious, she sprinted forward and leapt impossibly onto a chair with a missing leg. From there, she grabbed the note from amongst the thick books on an ancient bookshelf. Just as the red-eyed figure changed directions, she held the chair in front of her, blocking its way. She quickly found the exit and headed towards it. But it was too late. The mysterious figure caught her right in time, and she let out a deafening scream.

"Fiona!" Kaylie called out, but there was no answer.

At that moment, Excalibur, the sword of light and justice, shone as bright as the sun. There was a short pause before mighty sparks shot out of it, completely annihilating the cabin.

"Fiona," they all said with great relief.

"Yes, I'm back. But I found something interesting when I was in there chased by someone or something," Fiona replied, gazing at the big mark where the cabin used to be. She showed them a piece of parchment with small handwriting on it. Th note said,

Look for the jewelled crown,
Hidden to find.
Use for good,
Or it will badly blind.

It is greatly located
In the treacherous tower
Of dragons and death,
Where burning fire would shower.

CHAPTER 6

A RIDDLE

"It's a riddle," Ali pointed out as if no one else had noticed.

"Look for the jewelled crown? Oh, it means the crown of justice. If we find the crown, it can help us restore our and Magicland's magic," Fiona shared.

"'It is greatly located in the treacherous tower of dragons and death, where burning fire would shower.' So we know it's located in the dragon tower, 'where burning fire would shower.' It's in the place where he keeps his dragons," Lily added, simplifying the riddle.

"What we don't know is where he keeps them," Ali said with a sigh.

"Well then, we'll have to find out. Don't we?" Kaylie asked as she led them out of the old cave.

Unfortunately, the king of dragons had caught the dragon prisoners red-handed. He kept them in another dungeon, because the great Excalibur had wrecked the first one. Kaylie and the others raced to the castle and were thinking of a plan to break in. "What are we going to do?" asked Ali, the mythical phoenix.

"I don't know," Lily admitted as she saw dragons coming from every direction.

"Over there," Ali said, pointing to an open window. Outside was a long spiral staircase that passed through three dungeon floors. And there it was, the dragons' half of the tower. There was a big light-coloured dragon with eyes as bright as the sun. This was one frightened dragon. It was captured by the dragon master as he was the only one who committed evil. Or was he?

"How do we get up there?" asked Fiona. Even before she heard a word, she felt they were going to do the craziest thing ever.

Think straight, Kaylie, think straight, she thought, clenching Excalibur tightly in her hands.

After a flash of bright white, Kaylie, Lily, Fiona, and Ali were excited to see what was about to happen.

"Are we there yet?" questioned Kaylie, half opening her eyes to see what happened after the light merged with the clouds.

Nothing had happened, but a large piece of elastic had appeared. "What do we do with that? Do we just tie it to a tree or something and then catapult through the window? That would be crazy," Lily said with a joke but answering her own question at the same time.

"You're a genius, Lily. So that's what we're supposed to do with the elastic," Kaylie whispered as large fire-breathing dragons had appeared out of nowhere. Luckily, they did not spot them.

Ali tied the elastic to a tall grey tree with hardly any leaves, or any signs of life for that matter. Wobble, wobble. Kaylie made sure it was on tight, and they'd soon be zooming through the air thanks to the potential force of the rubber band.

"Ready, steady, aim, mark, set, ready to shoot—" Fiona started.

"Fire!" Kaylie interrupted, losing her patience with Fiona's rather too long ready-to-go line.

Saying the word "fire" made them fly through the open window. As soon as they got up, two apparently hungry dragons chased them up three flights of stairs. They'd reached the dragons' den. But was this the end of the heavy-footed dragons?

The stairs were right ahead, but an oversized dragon blocked the way. It breathed out a huge line of fire almost too close to the feathers on Ali's head.

As they zoomed across to the stairs on the other side, they slid under the dragon and somehow gaining speed, zoomed up the long spiral of stairs. Two more to go. With the dragons breathing fire while chasing after them, Kaylie, Lily, Fiona, and Ali ran faster than the world's fastest racing car up the stairs. One more to go, and they would be there. *Gggggrrrrrrrr. Roooooooaaaaaaaaaaarrrrrr.* The dragons were as angry as savage lions about to attack a herd of sheep.

"By the way, if you can understand me, do you always follow your master's rules because he is the dragon kingand he has way more power than you? Between us, I can tell you that he called you ugly and useless creatures, and that's not very nice, is it?" Lily added, cleverly deceiving them into thinking the dragon king had called them mean names. It seemed to work as the others joined them to hunt down the dragon king.

"Where is the crown?" asked Fiona.

"Over there in that cage with a real dragon in it," Ali answered, pointing to a very shy dragon that looked nothing like the rest. This dragon was pretty, shiny, and white with large eyes shaped like those of a cat. Her eyes were light-orange topaz colour. This dragon was extraordinary.

"How do we get it?" asked Lily, gazing at the innocent-looking dragon with great interest.

"Oh, I know what that is. It's a water dragon, of course. It can help us overthrow the dragon king," Ali said confidently. "We need to get it out of there to obliterate the tower of doom."

"It's harmless, right?" Lily asked.

"Of course it is harmless, if you don't hurt it," Ali assured Lily and the others.

The jewelled crown, stiff as a statue, stood hidden behind a large, furry, white tail with small blunt spikes. But no key was in sight to use to release the creature.

CHAPTER 7

THE EXCALIBUR OF LIGHT AND JUSTICE

As the sun had gotten warmer and warmer, and things somehow seemed more difficult to solve.

Roooaaaaaarr! A humungous fire-breathing dragon suddenly appeared, cornering them to the wall. It huffed and puffed, recharging its power. And then it blew.

When the fire came out of its mouth, Ali, Kaylie, Lily, and Fiona thought they were about to die.

Then suddenly, there was a flash, and the dragon became stiff as a statue. Its fire was extinguished, draining the dragon king's last bit of fire magic. The dragon looked as if it was paralysed.

Zap! Excalibur made things a lot easier. A fiery substance sprang out of its shiny metal body and made a hole in the cage large enough to fit a medium-sized water dragon and about eight people.

After the water dragon was saved, it became loyal to its rescuers. After Kaylie retrieved the jewelled crown of justice, the water dragon permitted them all to hop on its back. With its mighty wings high in the air and free as a bird, the water dragon flew. Fiery dragon after fiery dragon followed them, breathing out scorching fire. The king of the dragons appeared on what used to be the king of the dragons. He was so aggravated by Lily deceiving his dragons that he gave a loud shout and bellowed, "Get those prisoners and that dragon!"

"Wait, we can offer you a deal. You let us go, and we will give you this powerful crown," Lily bargained, showing the crown and expecting he hadn't known about it.

"The crown of justice? Give it to me, and I will let you go," the dragon king said while gaining interest.

"Deal." Lily agreed and threw the crown over to him as he lowered towards his dragon.

"Lily, no," they all cried with doom.

"Ha, ha, ha. Now that the power has come to me, I will ruin the human world," said the king of dragons.

At those words, the crown flashed. There was a shriek, and the sword glowed.

"I can't see," gasped the blinded man.

Kaboom! The great Excalibur forced itself through the ground, and the moment it touched the earth's surface, streams of light and magic flew all over Magicland and the dragon tower, generated life. Plant after plant of happy green enlightened the world. Emerald-green grass, light-blue rivers, and tall gold houses appeared.

All the dragon king's dragons were transformed into beautiful multicoloured creatures that were less harmful, if at all harmful.

This was not the end of the great story though. Unnoticed by the others, the dragon king blindly reached the sword and drained it of energy, life, and magic.

There were no more pretty and nice dragons in sight, no more greenness, no more free people in great gold houses. There was nothing. Nothing at all but dull grey and red fire.

"You will pay for this," shouted the dragon king with great fury.

"I don't think so," Kaylie replied, charging towards him to snatch the sword from him. But she didn't get there in time.

"The sword is mine, truly mine. I will destroy everything with its power, starting with you," the dragon king threatened.

Kaylie and the others took off on the water-breathing dragon, ready to bring back life. The great white dragon circled the sky, with its bright-orange topaz eyes gazing at the dragon king with caution. But as it was about to breathe out water, a huge stream of snow and ice showered down, attempting to spray him. But only one drop landed on his eye, which didn't matter to him.

"Quick, dragons, lead me to the tower where the death crown is at," the dragon king ordered. He assumed he would get there in time and transform the sword into the Excalibur of dragons and death, or the Excalibur of the dragon king. Who knew what he was going to call it? But was he going to reach there in time?

"Where is the crown? It can help us destroy him once and for all," Ali whispered.

"That means we have to go back and get it," Lily said.

Were they going to get the crown in time, or was the dragon king going to create his ultimate weapon with both the crown and Excalibur?

CHAPTER 8

THE FINAL BATTLE

Gliding down elegantly, the white water dragon dodged the evil king's fire dragons and reached its tiny little claws for the crown. It was much faster than any other dragon in sight, and it had a bigger wingspan to fly away faster.

On the other side, the evil king gradually approached his dragon-filled castle, his demon-red eyes flaming. The evil blind man laughed demonically as he sensed he was getting closer and closer to his evil lair.

Boom! Then suddenly, the dragon he was sitting on smashed the deathly walls of his fort, and its dark purple and orange wings had scooped the crown. Even the crown was dull and grey over here.

"No," they all shouted, except for Lily. Lily ran, dodging the flames of every dragon. Clenching the crown in her hand, she headed towards the king. What was she doing? That question ran across four minds and, of course, the minds of the scaly fiery dragons. She sent the crown flying like a projectile. It landed on the floor beside the king's ankle. She had missed! She was aiming for the two other items so it would connect, and the world would be saved.

"What's this?" he demanded.

"It's the crown of evil you're after," Kaylie lied.

"Yes, it's mine now!" confirmed the man as he grabbed hold of it.

Kaboom! A circle of gold light grew larger and larger. Kaylie, Lily, Fiona, and Ali—along with the water dragon—had defeated the dragon king once and for all. The dragons once again turned into beautiful multicoloured creatures. The bloody red of the dragon tower faded to a gorgeous white castle with delicate pink flowers dangling from the walls and across a never-ending steam of light blue. Freshly cut grass lay unharmed at every turn you took.

Wooden huts and houses stayed warm as their owners and the people of Magicland are welcomed in to do whatever they like and, most important, be free. In the greenness, smiling children ran around wildly as the adults prepared food for the upcoming festival. Traditionally, a festival was held if if the people were freed, and whoever freed them would be their leader.

"Is he dead?" asked Ali, flapping his mighty wings.

"I can use my powers now," Fiona proclaimed with happiness.

Lily and Kaylie both grew light-gold flared dragon wings. A magic staff the size of a tree and the width of a thick branch suddenly appeared in their hands as they were now the new leaders of Magicland. In the distance was Excalibur. It had drilled halfway through the rich soil and now grew light-pink flowers on its handle. It looked as though it had been there for years.

The former dragon king was no longer king of the dragons or of anyone or anything. He was sent to Magicland Prison, miles from view.

In the perfect warm weather, the festival began. Hundreds of people drank, ate, laughed, sang, and cheered. It was the best time of their lives.

Lily and Kaylie were both leaders of this land, but they missed their home too. They had to convince their mum, dad, and siblings to come and stay there as long as they lived.

They told everyone they'd return and then ran through the woods to their house. After they told their parents all about it, Mr James nearly fainted but stayed strong.

"We searched days for you, and you say you went to fairyland or something," Mr James said with a sigh.

"We want to go back. Why don't you come with us?" Lily suggested.

"I would love to," Ana exclaimed.

"I would love to more!" Layla said, trying to one-up her sister as usual..

"No, I would," Edward joined in.

"So where is this Magicland?" asked Dad with interest whilst Mum said nothing and froze.

"Follow us," Kaylie said, leading the way.

Minutes later, they were at the small cave hiding all the magic. When they had left there to tell their parents about the place, Lily's and Kaylie's wings and staffs had disappeared. Now, as the whole family wondered what on earth could be so magical in this cave and grew closer to a hidden world, the wings and staffs returned.

CHAPTER 9

A NEW WORLD AND A NEW LIFE

"Wow," Layla, Ana, and Edward exclaimed as they saw large wings sprouting from Lily's and Kaylie's backs and magical staffs clenched in their hands.

Dad was greatly amazed at this. Mum was okay with it and delighted.

"Is that our house?" Edward asked, pointing to a large castle surrounded by tiny houses.

"Yes, it is! And it's all thanks to Lily and Kaylie." Fiona smiled warmly as she joined the festival, soaring through the sky with excitement.

"So you're the leaders?" Dad questioned with greatness.

"Yes, we are," Kaylie said with a smile and showed her magical staff to her dad.

"There's no work or anything. So you're just free to do whatever you want?" asked Dad suspiciously.

"Um, I guess so," Kaylie answered, starting to feel annoyed.

"Yes! We're moving here everyone!" Dad said, jumping around. As he headed towards the castle, he asked if Kaylie or Lily could use their magical staffs to move everything from their house to the castle. He was so excited that he actually smashed his phone. He asked them to fix it.

"Well, that was easy," Lily said as she headed to the festival.

Hours and hours of never-ending fun and laughter passed. Except for the blinded man, who was once the dragon king. Well, in truth, he had healed his eyes with a powerful spell but pretended he was still blind. He needed to escape and fast. The evil man was left there alone, and the only prisoner, so he could think of a plan in peace. His first thought was to get the mighty Excalibur back.

"Ha, ha," the demon-like man chuckled evilly as he had the best plan to rule Magicland again.

The people of Magicland, as well as the new leaders, didn't know what was about to happen. But on the bright side, they were partying like crazy. When the sun went down, the sky was filled with tiny stars and a large moon

"Best day ever," they all shouted. Dad's shout was the loudest.

"Goodnight," Ali and Fiona called as they flew up to their windows.

This was truly the best day or days ever. They had another festival coming up with fun and laughter. They were going to stay there forever and as long as they lived. *Maybe it's time I shared my secret,* thought Mum as she went to bed.